Contents

There are 12 brilliant titles in the
Kitty and **friends** series.
Collect them all!

I don't want to!
I can't find it!
It's not fair!
But you promised!
Why not?
I know!
I'm scared!
I wish!
Why me?
I'm bored!
It's not my fault!
So what!

Why me?

Bel Mooney

Illustrated by Margaret Chamberlain

EGMONT

For Matthew and Rosie Johns

First published in Great Britain 1996
by Methuen Children's Books Limited

This edition published 2003 by Egmont Books Limited,
239 Kensington High Street, London W8 6SA

Text copyright © 1996 Bel Mooney
Illustrations copyright © 1996 Margaret Chamberlain

ISBN 1 4052 0383 8

1 3 5 7 9 0 8 6 4 2

A CIP catalogue record for this title
is available from the British Library

Printed in Great Britain
by Cox & Wyman Ltd, Reading, Berkshire

Why me?

. . . a bad luck day

'Hide, Kitty!' whispered Dan.

'Run for cover!' growled Dad.

'Why?' asked Kitty.

'Mum's in a *terrible* mood. She's in the worst mood since . . . since . . . the *whole history* of bad moods! She's on the rampage!' Daniel explained.

'Never mind, Dan – we can get out of the way. We've got to go and pick up the lawnmower from the menders,' grinned Dad.

'Take me too!' pleaded Kitty.

But it was too late. They went out of the door before Kitty could stop them, leaving her alone in the house with Mum. The terrible Mum. The Mum on the rampage.

Oh help, thought Kitty.

Then, Oh, it can't be as bad as they say.

Then, Oh help! again.

Because she heard Mum's feet walking to and fro upstairs, and it was a walk Kitty knew. It was a quick and bad-tempered walk. It said, 'I'm in a very bad mood and I'll get very cross with anybody who gets in my way.' It meant trouble.

Kitty had just decided that the safest place was the garden – even though it was just starting to rain – when Mum ran down the stairs and burst in through the kitchen door.

'Kitty! You're not going outside in this weather, are you?' she shouted.

'No, Mum,' said Kitty, closing the back door.

'Did you use any of my bubble bath last night?'

'No, Mum,' said Kitty.

'Well, somebody did,' Mum said crossly. 'And somebody must have pressed the button on our clock radio, because it went off much too early. Have you been messing about in my room?'

'No, Mum,' said Kitty.

'And by the way – I passed your bedroom and it's a terrible mess. Don't you think you're old enough to keep it tidy?'

Kitty and friends

'No, Mum,' said Kitty.

'Don't be cheeky, Kitty!' said Mum.

Kitty sat down at the kitchen table and rested her chin on her hands. She didn't say anything for a few minutes – just watched Mum banging about the kitchen putting things away.

Why me?

'Mum?' she said at last. 'Why are you in a bad mood?'

'I'm not in a bad mood!' snapped Mum.

'No, Mum,' said Kitty.

It simply wasn't fair, she thought. When your Mum and Dad were in a bad mood you just had to put up with it, but when you were in a bad mood they said you were naughty or cheeky. Typical of grown-ups!

'I have to do everything in this house,' Mum moaned, as she wiped the draining board, 'and nobody helps. And when everything goes wrong, nobody cares.'

'What's gone wrong, Mum?' asked Kitty.

'First the wretched clock. Then no bubble bath. Then I put my finger through my only pair of decent tights. Then I dropped a whole bottle of milk, didn't I? Then your father tells me he's going out with Dan, when I wanted to use the car to go to the hairdressers. Then I couldn't find one of my gold hoop ear-rings, and I've looked *everywhere* . . . Added to that, the whole house is a mess, and you and Daniel don't do anything to help, and I'm fed up having to run round after you all . . .'

'So it's a bad mood day!' said Kitty brightly.

'That's not very helpful, Kitty,' said Mum. 'It's a bad luck day, more like it!'

'Well, at least you're going to get your hair done,' said Kitty, 'so that will cheer you up.'

'Oh yes, when it's raining, and I've got to go on the bus! Anyway, I don't know what to do with stupid hair like mine – I'm so bored with it,' moaned Mum.

That was the moment when Kitty decided she had done all she could to get Mum in a good mood. 'I'll just go upstairs and start tidying my room,' she said sweetly, as she walked out the door.

Why me?

'No! You'll have to go next door till Dad gets back,' said Mum.

Can't do anything right, thought Kitty. But she said, 'Have a nice time at the hairdresser, Mum!' and ran happily over to William's.

Much later, Dad telephoned to say he and Dan were back, and so Kitty came home. She told Daniel and Dad what Mum had said about having too much to do, so they all got busy and gave the house a good tidy. It looked much better, and Kitty felt pleased. They were all in the kitchen having tea and biscuits when they heard the front door slam.

'Mum's back,' said Dan.

'Hallo, love!' called Dad.

'We're in the kitchen,' Kitty shouted.

But Mum ran upstairs, and they heard the bathroom door slam. Then silence.

'Oh dear, something's wrong,' whispered Dad.

'Let me sort it out,' said Kitty.

She went upstairs and stopped outside the bathroom door. She thought she heard a snuffling noise from inside, as if someone was crying.

'Mum?' she called, worried.

'Go away!' came the reply.

'Let me in – please, Mum.'

'No . . . Oh . . . it looks *terrible* . . . and I only wanted a change,' cried Mum.

'PLEASE let me in!' said Kitty

After a few minutes she heard the bolt being pulled back, and the door opened. She walked in – and couldn't believe her eyes. Mum was sitting unhappily on the edge of the bath. Her eyes were bright red – but so was her hair! What's more, it was in a strange wild style – sort of sticking up on top, with gel. Kitty stared and stared. The she said, 'WOW!'

Why me?

Mum got up and glared into the bathroom mirror.

'Look at it!' she wailed. 'I just wanted a hint of colour, and they've turned me into a carrot! It's terrible! Oh – why did they have to do it to *me*?'

Then she started to cry again.

'I know why they did it to you, Mum,' said Kitty.

'Wh . . . wh . . . why?' sobbed Mum.

'To make you look young and with-it, of course!' said Kitty cheerfully. 'Now, just you come with me!'

She grabbed Mum by the hand and dragged her into the big bedroom. Then, she plonked her down in front of her dressing table and said, 'Start putting your make-up on.'

'Why?' asked Mum, reaching for the eye-shadow.

But Kitty didn't take any notice. She was opening the wardrobe, and looking in drawers, and pulling out the old suitcase from under the bed, where she knew Mum and Dad kept clothes they hadn't worn for years, but didn't want to give away.

Then she heard Dad coming up and quickly slammed the door. As Mum started to put eye make-up on, Kitty shouted, 'Give us ten minutes, Dad – then we'll have a surprise for you!' Then she set to work . . .

Not long afterwards Dad and Daniel were in the sitting room, waiting, when Kitty opened the door, and made a noise like a trumpet.

Why me?

'Da-daa, da-daa,' she went, standing aside to let Mum walk by her into the room.

Dad stared – as if his eyes would pop out of his head. Daniel's mouth dropped open, so that he looked like a goldfish. Then Dad said one word: 'WOW!'

Mum stood there, with her new red hair in the really modern style – and she looked wonderful. Kitty had found the grey suede mini-skirt she hadn't worn for years, and the black leather biker's jacket she wore when she was going out with Dad, and shiny black tights, and some soft black leather ankle boots she had bought in a sale then not worn, because she said 'they're too young for me'.

'What have you done, love? You look like a teenager!' said Dad.

'I like the hair, Mum! All the boys in school will think you're my big sister,' said Dan, reaching up to stroke her head gently.

'You know, I always did like red-heads,' said Dad, slipping an arm around her waist.

'Do you remember when I first wore this jacket?' whispered Mum, giving him a soppy look.

'Could I ever forget?' he whispered, giving her one back.

Kitty and Dan started to walk away, grinning at each other. But Kitty couldn't resist turning round to have the last word.

'Now you know why the hairdresser chose *you*, Mum,' she said.

'Why's that, then?' smiled Mum.

'So Dad would remember his good luck when *you* chose *him*!' said Kitty.

Why me?

. . . Rosie's grandma

One day Rosie invited Kitty to stay at her house. Kitty was very excited, because it had never happened before. Rosie had a big family, and so her Mum said there was no room for visitors.

'Why has she changed her mind?' asked Kitty.

'I asked her too many times!' Rosie grinned. 'But you'll have to sleep on the floor.'

'That's fun!' said Kitty.

'Friday then,' Rosie said, 'you bring your stuff to school.'

On Friday morning Kitty packed her pyjamas and washing things in a small bag, then looked at Mr Tubs. She hated leaving him behind, but Rosie had a big sister called Sara who was very smart and grown-up . . .

'She might laugh at you, Mr Tubs,' whispered Kitty, tucking the old bear into her bed.

The day seemed to go very slowly. Usually Kitty liked Miss Robinson's lessons, but today they dragged. She wanted the weekend to start, so she could get to Rosie's house. So she didn't want to learn about the Romans at all!

At last it was home time. Rosie's Mum was at the school gate, and they walked the four streets it took to get to Rosie's house. From upstairs came the sound of

Why me?

Sam's guitar. He was Rosie's oldest brother, and wore his hair in long dreadlocks, like heavy ropes, and played guitar in a band. From the sitting room came the sound of the television, and Kitty waved to Robbie and Ben, who lounged on the floor watching. Robbie was fourteen and Ben was sixteen, and Kitty thought them very handsome!

Just then Sara rushed in, scattering books and nearly knocking Rosie over.

'Watch where you're going!' yelled Rosie.

'Shouldn't be in the way, should you, Squirt?' Sara snapped.

Kitty and friends

Kitty didn't like that. Oh, please don't let them start quarrelling, she thought. It was always so embarrassing, when you went to somebody's house, if the family started arguing.

But Sara ran upstairs to the room she shared with Rosie, and soon the sound of loud rap music joined the rest. Kitty liked all the noise. It made her own house seem very quiet.

The girls watched some television, then played Snakes and Ladders. Then suddenly there was a lot more noise – and Rosie's Dad and Grandma came in through the front door, laughing very loudly as if someone had just told a joke.

Rosie rushed to give them a kiss, and Kitty followed shyly. She liked Rosie's Mum and Dad, but didn't really know Grandma – who had only arrived the week

Why me?

before from Jamaica, where she lived.

'Kitty!' she said with a big grin. 'Now that's a nice name. But you should have a long tail and whiskers, girl!'

'Then she'd be a mouse!' shrieked Rosie's Mum.

Kitty felt a bit silly. Why are they making jokes about *me*? she thought. But they were all looking at her, smiling broadly – so she had to smile back.

It was funny – being at somebody else's house. You didn't know what to do, or how to be. After a while you got tired of smiling all the time and being polite. That was how Kitty started to feel, by the time it was time for supper.

There was a delicious smell of fried chicken, all through the house. From the kitchen came a clatter of cooking and a shouting as Rosie's Mum and Grandma talked to each other. Her Dad was laying the table. They all seemed to be rushing.

Rosie explained it was because her Mum had to go out to her evening job, and her Dad was going to a meeting at his Club.

'Supper will be good, Kit. My Gran's a great cook.'

It was one of the best meals Kitty had tasted for a long time. There was fried chicken with a sort of crust on it, and rice, and sweet potato mashed up with butter, and a strange green vegetable called okra, which looked like fingers. For afters they had baked bananas and ice cream . . .

As they ate busily it seemed that everybody talked at once. Sam was telling Sara that his band had been booked for a really good gig, and Robbie and Ben were telling their Dad about a football match, and Rosie was trying to persuade her Mum to buy her some new trainers. All the time Grandma was passing things across the table, and offering more, and smiling all the time. Still, Kitty felt a bit afraid of

Why me?

her – although she didn't know why.

'You like my food, girl?' she asked.

Kitty nodded shyly, her mouth full.

'Better than cat food – eh?' laughed Grandma, and suddenly they were all quiet – and joined in. So Kitty felt silly again. She decided secretly she didn't really like Rosie's Grandma.

When the meal was over everybody got up at once. 'Now, we're both off out,' said Rosie's Mum loudly, 'and Grandma's going upstairs to rest. So I'm going to give you – Sam – the job of organising the clearing up.'

'Why me?' asked Sam.

'You're the oldest, that's why! And you'd better get in practice, so you make some girl a good husband one of these days!' said Rosie's Mum.

Sam just grunted. And when the front door had banged behind Rosie's parents, and Grandma had left the room, he stood by the table with his arms folded.

'OK – Ma said I had to organise the clearing up, not DO it!' he said. 'So Sara – it's your job.'

'Why me?' shouted Sara.

'Because you're a girl!' said Sam.

'Oh! . . . of all the stupid things to say! That's it! I'm off round to Vick's place!' And before anyone could stop her, Sara rushed out of the room, very crossly.

'Well, it looks like you guys!' said Sam, pointing at Robbie and Ben.

'Hard luck!' grinned Robbie. 'We've got a team practice, and you know how

Why me?

much Dad cares about that!' So, looking very pleased with themselves, they left too.

'OK then Rosie – it's you,' sighed Sam.

'Why me?' yelled Rosie.

'Because you're the youngest,' said Sam.

'Why not YOU?' wailed Rosie.

'Look, I've got a band rehearsal. I can't be late. It's too important, can't you see? Tell you what, I'll give you a pound tomorrow, if you're good.'

With that he strolled out, leaving Rosie looking gloomily at all the dirty plates.

'A pound's not much for this lot,' she said. 'And I wanted to watch that game programme, didn't you?'

To tell the truth, Kitty didn't feel at all like helping Rosie wash up, so she nodded.

'Anyway, you're a visitor,' said Rosie, 'so you can't do it. And it's too much for me. Come on, Kit – we'll go and watch TV.'

'What if your Mum or Dad comes back early?'

'Sam will get into trouble,' grinned Rosie.

They went into the sitting room, and closed the door tightly – as if that way all the washing up could be kept outside.

The television was turned up very loudly, and the programme was very funny so that soon Kitty and Rosie forgot about the dirty dishes altogether, and were roaring with laughter. But after a while Kitty thought she heard a clinking sound from the back of the house. She asked Rosie if she heard it, but Rosie just giggled at the screen, and shook her head. So Kitty got up quietly, and left the room.

In the kitchen Rosie's Grandma was filling the sink full of soapy water. All the dirty plates, and pans and dishes were stacked on the side, and she had her sleeves rolled up to the elbow. She smiled at Kitty.

'Soon have this lot cleared away!' she said cheerfully.

Why me?

Kitty looked at the mess, and asked, 'But why are you doing it?'

'Why *not*, girl? Somebody's got to!'

'But you cooked. My Dad says the one that cooks shouldn't wash up,' Kitty said.

'This is my *family* – so why wouldn't I cook for them all, and wash it up too?'

'Shall I help you?'

'Why, that would be a kind thing, little Kitty-girl!' said Grandma.

They set to work, and as she washed and Kitty dried, Rosie's Grandma told Kitty wonderful stories from Jamaica. She told her about magic hummingbirds, and goats and snakes, and butterflies as big as your hand, and secret herb medicines that could cure even a scorpion's sting. And she hummed songs with no words, that reminded Kitty a bit of Sam's guitar. She made Kitty want to dance.

At last Rosie came out into the kitchen. 'So there you are, Kit!' she said. 'I thought you must have gone upstairs to read or something.' Then she looked round, and just said 'Oh . . .' Then, looking a bit ashamed, she asked, 'Why did you two do all the washing up?'

'Because me and Kitty-the-Cat – we wanted to have a party!' said Grandma, giving Kitty a hug that took all her breath away.

'Yes,' squeaked Kitty, 'and we thought,

Why me?

why not just us?'

And the funny thing was, the nicest thing about staying with Rosie turned out to be that time in the kitchen with Grandma.

But do you think they told Rosie's Mum and Dad what had happened?

Why me?

... William and the bad seeds

William's mother and father were mad about gardening, and William caught the craze as well.

'I've been given my own bit of garden, Kit,' he said proudly. 'It's going to be better than anybody's. And our garden's going to be much better than your garden!'

'I suppose it is,' said Kitty in a cool voice. She hated it when people said things like that. It was silly.

Why me?

That's why she pretended not to be interested when William showed her the little trowel he had bought with his pocket money, and three packets of seeds.

'What are you going to grow – roses, or dandelions?' Kitty asked in a not-very-nice voice.

'I don't want to grow *flowers* – flowers are for wimps,' said William. 'I'm going to grow potatoes and tomatoes and peas. Then I'll be able to make myself a meal!'

Kitty thought that sounded like a very good idea, but she didn't want to say so. She watched in silence as William took the big spade, and started to dig over his patch of garden. He huffed and puffed, and asked her if she wanted to help, but she shook her head. She watched as he raked the soil finely, then knelt and made little lines in it with his trowel.

'That's where you put the seeds,' he explained.

Kitty thought he sounded like someone who knows everything, and it annoyed her. 'Don't you have to have special bags for tomatoes?' she asked.

'What do you mean?'

'I've seen a picture somewhere. Special bags inside a greenhouse, and the tomatoes grow up the side.'

'No,' said William.

'And for peas too,' said Kitty.

'What do you mean?' asked William.

'I don't know . . . I thought peas had to grow up special pole-things. And is it the right time of year to put the seeds in?'

'Of course it is,' said William.

'Let me see the packets,' said Kitty, holding out her hand.

'NO!' shouted William. 'I know how to do it, so there!'

'Well, I think you ought to ask your

Why me?

Dad,' said Kitty in her most annoying voice
– the one that said, 'Aren't you a silly boy?'

William went red and said, 'Why don't
you mind your own business, Kitty? So
Kitty just shrugged, and crawled back into
her own garden through the hole in the
fence – and that was that.

A week passed. Every couple of days
Kitty stood on tiptoe and looked over the
fence to see how William's garden grew. In
her heart she wanted nothing to happen
– because she was cross with him for being
such a know-all. But when she saw him she
asked sweetly, 'How are the plants coming
on, Will?'

The first week he answered, 'It's too
soon, silly!' The second week he said the
same. But when it got to the third week he
changed the tone of his voice. 'Er . . .
nothing's happened yet,' he mumbled.
Which Kitty knew already, because she
had been watching.

Kitty and friends

One Saturday morning, exactly four weeks after William had planted his seeds, Kitty crawled through the hole in the fence and found him looking down at his little garden. There was one little green shoot in the middle of the patch of soil – that's all. Suddenly Kitty wanted this to be one of his plants. She grinned and pointed and said, 'There you are! Something's growing!'

But William just shook his head and frowned. 'No, Kit – that's just a weed. Look . . .' And he bent down and pulled up the little shoot of dandelion – for that's

Why me?

what it was. 'You said I should grow dandelions, Kitty,' he said sadly.

Kitty felt sorry for him. 'I was only kidding,' she said, 'and listen, Will – I'm sure your seeds will grow. You've got to give them time.'

'Just look at it!' William said, pointing to the bare earth. '*Nothing*'s going to grow!'

'Maybe you got some packets of bad seeds, just by accident,' said Kitty.

'Why me?' William sighed. 'And I used up all my pocket money too.'

'It could have happened to anybody,' said Kitty.

'Maybe I'm just bad at gardening,' said William in a *very* gloomy voice.

'No – definitely bad seeds,' said Kitty, 'not your fault at all.'

William didn't want to play. He just picked up his new trowel and walked into his house, looking so disappointed Kitty wanted to cry.

Crying doesn't do any good, though, she thought to herself. I should be able to come up with a plan . . .

She went back into her house, went upstairs, and opened up her money box. 'Hmm . . . not bad,' she said, as she counted the coins.

A little later Kitty asked her father to take her to the garden centre. She had such a good idea! But when they got to the garden centre, and she asked the man if they could sell her some little tomato and potato and pea plants, he shook his head.

'We don't sell them already grown,' he said, 'only flowers. You've got to grow vegetables from seed, love.'

'I thought he might say that, Kitty,' said Dad , as they walked away.

Now Kitty always liked to get her own

Why me?

way, and she didn't see why her plan shouldn't work. Whatever happened, she had to make William feel better. So she stopped suddenly, stamped her foot, and turned round. 'We're going back, Dad,' she said, 'because I don't get beaten that easily – not me!'

Later Kitty went to have tea with William, and found him feeling very sorry for himself. 'Dad's been teasing me about my plants,' he said, 'and it's not fair. Why do grown-ups always have to tease?'

'Because they like to think they're cleverer than us,' said Kitty, 'but they're sometimes wrong, aren't they?'

'Not this time,' said William, 'Dad says I've got black fingers, and he's right.'

'Don't be so sure,' said Kitty, in a knowing voice.

That night, when it was dark, Kitty crept outside with Daniel. She had let him into her secret because she needed his help.

They went down to the garden shed to get some things, and then back and through the hole in the fence. Then Dan stood by holding the torch steady, whilst Kitty set to work. Neither of them spoke, but every so often they looked up at William's house. The lights were on, but nobody came out into the garden.

Kitty woke up early next morning. She pulled her curtains aside and looked out. It was a bright sunny day. William's garden was empty. 'Oh, please, please come out and see!' muttered Kitty. But nobody did.

At last she grew tired of waiting and went downstairs. Mum was cooking scrambled eggs. 'Go and call Daniel and Dad,' she said. So they were all in the kitchen eating when there was a loud knock on the back door.

'Kitty! Kitty!' yelled William.

Kitty just had time to give Dan the tiniest, tiniest wink before William burst in.

Why me?

'Come and see! Come and see!' he said.

'See what?' Kitty asked.

'My garden! There's things growing in it!' shouted William excitedly. 'Come on!'

Kitty followed him back through the fence, and into his own garden. His Mum and Dad were standing looking at his own patch of earth – where, sure enough, there were six rows of green shoots.

'I don't understand it,' said William's Dad, shaking his head, 'they don't look anything like peas, or potatoes or tomatoes, Will.'

'What do they look like, then?' asked William.

'Well, those are busy lizzies, and those are . . . er . . . nasturtiums, and those are . . . I'm not sure . . .'

'Sweet peas?' said Kitty.

'That's right! How did did you guess, Kitty, you clever thing?' asked William's Dad.

'Oh . . . er . . . my Dad grew some last year,' said Kitty quickly.

'But how come they're all growing here,' said William, 'when I didn't plant them?'

'That's easy,' said Kitty, 'you didn't buy bad seeds, after all – they just made a mistake, and put the wrong pictures on the packets.'

'Can that happen?' William asked, as if he didn't believe it.

His Mum and Dad were staring at Kitty, in a way that made her think they knew something. She just stared back, until they smiled.

'Yes, Will, anything can happen when you're gardening,' said William's Dad, ruffling his hair.

'Now the real skill will be to make these tiny plants grow big and strong,' said William's Mum.

Why me?

'Oh, I can do that, all right!' said William happily.

When his Mum and Dad had gone inside William turned to Kitty and asked, 'Do seeds always grow up this big overnight?'

'Oh yes!' said Kitty. 'But then, I don't know as much about gardening as you, Will!'

'I wonder why I should get the wrong pictures on the packets . . . I mean, why *me*?' asked William thoughtfully.

'Because *I* don't like veggy-troubles and now you'll be able to give me a bunch of flowers instead!' Kitty said.

Why me?

. . . Anita's party

One day Anita came to school with a little pile of white envelopes, and quietly gave them out to ten of her friends. Of course, Kitty and Rosie were included.

Kitty tore hers open in a flash, and said, 'Hurray! Anita's having a party! What do you want for a birthday present, Anita?'

Anita shook her head. 'I don't know . . . Just come to my party,' she smiled. 'And you can help organise the games. You're good at that, aren't you, Kitty?'

'That's 'cos I'm so bossy!' grinned Kitty.

'Too right!' said Rosie.

Then the three friends laughed, linked arms and went into the classroom.

Kitty looked forward to the party SO much. There was something so magical about arriving at a friend's house, feeling a bit nervous (although you never knew why) and knowing there would be lights and lumpy parcels to pass and musical chairs and lovely sticky food and the birthday cake with its flickering candles and then (usually) the going-home bag full of goodies.

Not many of their class had parties. Kitty's Mum explained that it was because it costs quite a lot of money for all those little going-home bags, and so not every family could afford it. So that just made the parties that did happen all the more special. That's why Kitty looked forward to Anita's SO much.

Why me?

The great party was going to be on Saturday. On the Monday of that week Kitty felt fine. She knew she was well because she told her Mum she didn't want to eat her breakfast, and she told her teacher she didn't want to do her sums, and she yelled 'It's not fair!' at break time because big Tom wouldn't give her a piece of chewing gum but gave William one . . . All this showed that Kitty was FINE.

But on Tuesday she had a funny feeling in her neck, and that made her quieter than usual. By Wednesday the feeling had moved down to her throat, and on Thursday her poor chest felt as if it was on fire and she couldn't stop coughing.

'Poor old Kit,' said Mum, stroking her head, 'you'll have to stay off school today.'

'I don't want to!' croaked Kitty.

'What?' said Mum. 'Don't be silly! Usually you'd take any excuse to stay off school, and today you're really poorly.'

'No I'm not,' spluttered Kitty, before she began to cough and cough.

Mum got up, saying she was going to ring her job to say she wouldn't be in that day because she had to look after Kitty. As she walked across Kitty's bedroom, she spotted a brightly coloured card standing up on Kitty's table. She saw the word 'Party' – and remembered.

'So that's it!' she whispered to herself.

By the end of Thursday Kitty was worse, and on Friday morning she was a really sad sight. Her head ached, her throat was sore, and she had a pain in her chest – from coughing so much. Mum dosed her with red cough mixture, and gave her soothing sweets to suck, and sat in her room trying to cheer her up by playing games . . . but nothing could stop Kitty feeling miserable.

VERY miserable.

So miserable, that when Mum went

Why me?

downstairs to make her some hot black-currant juice, Kitty turned to cuddle Mr Tubs and made him all wet with her tears.

'Why me? Why me?' she sobbed. 'Why did I have to get ill this week, of all weeks? Why couldn't the cough have waited until after Anita's party?'

But by the time Mum came back Kitty was sitting up (looking very red in the face) and trying, very hard, to look better.

'If I'm better tomorrow morning – do you think I'll be able to go to Anita's party?' she asked hopefully.

Mum just looked at her, smiled, and shook her head sadly. 'Oh, Kitty love . . . I'm afraid it would take a bit of a miracle,' she said, 'but we'll see!'

'Why do grown-ups always say *We'll see*?' groaned Kitty.

'Because we don't know how things will be!' smiled Mum.

That night Daniel was unusually kind

to Kitty, and played a card game with her, and Dad sat on her bed and read her a story. But Kitty didn't feel better. She felt very sorry for herself indeed.

Saturday was the day of Anita's party, and when Kitty woke up she tried to make herself feel better. She got out of bed, put her dressing gown on, and started to go downstairs. But halfway down the stairs she started coughing really badly, so that Mum came out of the kitchen and called out, 'What are you doing up?'

'I think I'm better,' Kitty spluttered.

'No, you're not! You go back to bed this minute, my girl!' said Mum.

It was no good. Kitty knew she couldn't pretend. She was ill and she was going to miss Anita's party, and that was that.

'Why me, Mum?' she

Why me?

said, when Mum brought up her breakfast on a tray.

'You mean you'd rather the cough had chosen Rosie?' asked Mum.

'Yes . . . But that sounds a bit mean, doesn't it?' said Kitty.

'A tiny bit!' said Mum.

'Well, I wouldn't really want Rosie to be ill,' said Kitty.

'Or any of the others?'

'No-o,' said Kitty, thoughtfully.

'Well then!' said Mum – as if they had decided something, even though Kitty wasn't sure what.

The day dragged and dragged. By late afternoon, Kitty was starting to feel a little bit better, but knew there was no point in trying to tell her Mum she was well enough to go to the party.

When it came to the time Kitty knew the children would be arriving at Anita's house, she felt really sad. She imagined the paper hats, and the sound of music, and Anita opening all her presents, and Mrs Attra hitching up her lovely purple sari and clapping her hands to organise the first game.

'I should be there to help,' Kitty muttered, feeling cross.

Three hours went by. It was dark outside now, and Kitty's Mum came up to draw her curtains.

'I'm sorry you're so disappointed, love,' she said.

'So am I,' Kitty replied, in a sulky voice.

Just then the doorbell rang. Kitty heard her Dad's footsteps going down the hall to answer it, then the sound of voices, then her Dad laughing, then somebody saying, 'Shhh.'

'What's happening?' said Mum, going out on to the landing to look over the banisters.

Then she turned back, smiling all over

her face. 'Guess what, Kit? You've got a surprise!' she said happily.

Kitty was just pulling herself up in bed, when a lot of people burst into the room. First came Anita, then her Mum and Dad, then her three little brothers. They were each carrying something. Dad

and Daniel and Mum all stood by the door.

'If Kitty can't come to the party . . .'
Mr Attra began.

'Then the party must come to Kitty!'
Mrs Attra finished.

'I didn't want you to feel left out,' said
Anita, looking a bit shy.

'Can we play a game?' squealed her
three little brothers. Anita's Mum
explained that they wouldn't stay long as
it was way past the little boys' bedtime,
and they didn't want to make Kitty tired.
So Kitty's Mum asked Dan to take Anita's
brothers downstairs, and put on a cartoon
video to keep them quiet.

'Did you have a nice party?' asked Kitty.

'Yes, but it would have been better if
you'd been there,' said Anita.

'We needed you to help with the
games!' said Mrs Attra.

'You should have heard William yell
when we were playing Musical Chairs and

Why me?

he missed the chair and fell on his bottom!' giggled Anita.

'Such a noisy lot of kids!' grinned Mr Attra.

They all laughed. Then Dad got some chairs, and Anita and her parents started to push little parcels at Kitty.

First came the silver food containers. There were poppadums in one and some chicken tikka and rice in another, and (best of all) sticky Indian sweets in the third. 'Ohh, thank you!' Kitty cried.

Anita gave her a piece of the chocolate birthday cake, wrapped in a pink paper napkin, and two packets of crisps which, she said, were left over.

Then she handed Kitty a bag decorated with cartoon characters. 'Here's your going-home bag,' she said.

Kitty put her hand in the bag, feeling very excited. There were two packets of sweets, a rubber shaped like a car, a pencil, a biro, a key ring shaped like a pair of handcuffs, a packet of chewing gum, and a little notebook with a teddy bear on the front.

'Oh, thank you!' said Kitty again.

'She hasn't finished yet,' Mrs Attra smiled.

Then Anita put a large parcel, wrapped in pretty paper, into Kitty's hand.

'What's this?' Kitty asked.

'In India we have a custom which says if you are ill, every day is your birthday,' said Mr Attra.

'Is that true?' asked Kitty.

'No – silly!' said Anita. 'Just open it and don't ask questions.'

Why me?

Kitty undid the blue ribbon, pulled off the pretty paper, and parted the tissue paper to show – a beautiful Indian bedspread, patterned all over with blue and green elephants. And there was a matching cushion cover, decorated with tiny mirrors that caught the light.

'Oh . . . oh . . . it's . . . so lovely,' gasped Kitty, '. . . but it's your birthday not mine!'

'Ah, but *you* deserve a special present,' said Anita.

Kitty shook her head. 'Why me?' she asked.

'Because *you're* my very special friend,' said Anita.

Why me?

. . . why you?

Daniel was sitting having a boiled egg for his breakfast, when Kitty burst into the kitchen, waving an envelope.

'You've got a letter!' she said. 'Somebody's *written* to you!'

'No!' said Dan, in a silly, sarcastic voice. 'I thought a letter meant they'd sung me a song!'

'Very funny,' said Kitty.

'Now kids, don't start arguing,' said

Why me?

Mum, popping Kitty's egg into the pan.

Daniel took the letter, stared at his name on it, looked at the stamp, then turned it over.

'Well – aren't you going to open it?' said Kitty.

She thought her brother was very annoying. She also felt jealous of him for getting a letter. But that was nothing to how she was about to feel . . .

'Hey! I've won a prize!' yelled Daniel. 'Mum! Dad! I've won a prize!'

Mum came over and took the letter from him. Dad rushed into the room, and they both read the piece of paper.

'It was that writing competition!' said Mum.

'Was it the one at the bookshop?' asked Dad.

'Yes – and I wrote a poem,' said Dan, in a very excited voice.

'It says you won third prize!' said Mum, giving him a hug.

'Who's a clever old thing then?' grinned Dad.

'I get a book token and a certificate,' said Daniel.

'You'll have to stick it up on your wall,' said Mum.

'It's brilliant! I'm really proud of you,' said Dad. And he gave Dan a hug too.

Kitty was very quiet as she watched all this. Then she said, 'What about my egg?'

'Oh, sorry pet – I forgot,' said Mum, running back to the stove.

Dad and Daniel took no notice. They still were too busy looking at the letter.

'What was your poem about, Dan?' Dad asked.

'It was about trees,' said Dan.

'Lovely!' said Dad.

Kitty watched glumly as Mum neatly took the top off the boiled egg.

Why me?

'It's hard,' said Kitty crossly, 'and you didn't make me any soldiers!'

'What's the matter with you, cross-patch?' asked Dad.

Kitty looked at them all, and frowned a really terrible frown. Then she pushed her plate away quickly so that the egg fell over, and the knife dropped on the floor.

'I'd have *thought* you'd have guessed,' she said. 'I'd have *thought* that anybody who cared about anybody *else* in a family might have stopped for *just a minute* and wondered how *Kitty* was feeling.'

'What are you on about?' said Dan.

'Oh nothing. It's just that I went in for that competition too,' said Kitty – trying very hard to keep the wobble out of her voice.

'Oh,' said Mum.

'Oh dear,' said Dad.

'What was your poem about, dear?' asked Mum.

'It was about . . . er . . . about . . . a nice flower,' mumbled Kitty, 'like HIS was about silly old trees.'

'I'd forgotten you went in for it too,' said Dan.

'Why did HE win a prize? Why didn't I win one?' yelled Kitty.

'Oh, love . . .' Mum began.

'Why YOU, Daniel?' Kitty said. 'My poem was just as good as your poem.'

'I'm sure it was, pet,' said Dad. He sounded very unhappy.

'Why ME? Because I'm a genius, that's why!' crowed Daniel.

'Don't make her feel worse, Dan,' said Mum, quietly.

'Well, she's just trying to spoil things for me,' said Dan in a sulky voice.

'I'm afraid that's true,' sighed Dad.

'You've got to learn, Kitty, that not everybody can win,' said Mum.

That was too much for Kitty. She

Why me?

jumped up from the table, so that her chair crashed down on to the floor, and shouted, 'You're all on Daniel's side! Nobody cares about ME!' Then she ran out of the kitchen slamming the door behind her.

Upstairs in her room, Kitty cried and cried. She threw Mr Tubs on the floor in a temper – then felt very bad, and picked him up, and hugged him tightly.

'It's not fair, Mr Tubs,' she whispered.

Mr Tubs just looked at her with his wise old eyes. He knew.

Kitty pulled open her table drawer, rummaged around, and at last found what she was looking for. It was the notebook she had written her poem in. Kitty thought at first she would rip it into a hundred pieces. But Mr Tubs was looking at her, so she changed her mind.

She was just looking sadly at her poor old poem, when there was a knock on the door, and before she could yell, 'Go away!' it opened – and there was Dad.

'Hallo, old thing,' he said.

Kitty quickly shoved the book back into her drawer, but it was too late. 'What have you got there?' Dad asked.

'Nothing – it's private!' muttered Kitty.

'Well if it's nothing it can't be private, can it?' smiled Dad. 'Hey – is it your lovely poem, by any chance?'

'It's not a lovely poem,' said Kitty, in a very small voice.

'Let's see,' said Dad, holding out his hand.

At first Kitty didn't want to hand over her notebook. But Dad said 'please' with

Why me?

such a nice look on his face, that she did.

'Is this the poem?' he asked.

Kitty nodded. Then she couldn't bear to sit there while he read her poem, so rushed out. After less than five minutes she crept back.

She heard Dad laughing even before she went into her room. His chuckle was a lovely warm sound – and it went on and on. It made Kitty start to smile, even though she didn't really want to.

'What are you laughing at, Dad?' she asked, standing next to him.

'This!' he said, waving her book.

'Oh,' she said, sounding a bit hurt.

'Isn't it meant to be funny?' he asked.

'Well . . . yes.'

'It's wonderful!' spluttered Dad. 'Really brilliant!'

'Why didn't it win a prize then?' Kitty asked.

'Oh, that's easy,' said Dad. 'Don't you

see, Kit-Kat, that this isn't the *sort* of poem the people who pick winners would choose, in a proper writing competition? Dan's poem is about trees and the way they change as the seasons change, and it's lovely. It's also just the kind of poem you'd *expect* to win a prize. But your poem is really different. It's naughty and funny – like you!'

'But it's telling children *not* to be naughty!' Kitty protested.

'I know – it's an old-fashioned warning tale,' smiled Dad.

'But you really like it?' Kitty asked.

'Yes I do! So much that *I'm* going to give you a prize. I'll take you to the bookshop when Dan goes for his, and I'll buy you two books. OK?'

'What about a certificate then?' asked Kitty, with a cheeky smile.

Kitty's rose poem

There once was a girl called Rose,

Who had an enormous nose;

She had the worst habit,

Just like a little rabbit –

She picked and picked her nose!

She picked all night, she picked all day,

She picked it even during play,

Did Rose.

Her Mum and Dad said, 'Rose you're bad!'

They were ashamed! They felt so sad.

Her nose began to get a hole,

But still she dug just like a mole!

She cried, 'Why me?'

She was a sight to see,

But still she did not stop.

Her brother said, 'Oh you are dumb,
To pick your nose, not suck your thumb.'
Then one day she woke,
And before she spoke,
Her hand went to her nose.
But Rose got a shock,
For there was no nose...
So don't YOU be like disgusting Rose!

Kitty

Why me?

... Kitty hears some news

Mum and Dad had been acting very strangely for a couple of weeks now. Kitty didn't understand it at all. First, she found Mum crying in the sitting room.

'Oh, Mum, have you and Dad had a row?' Kitty asked. Right away, Mum's tears stopped, and she gave a big bright smile. 'Oh no, love,' she said, 'that's the *last* . . .'

Next, Mum was on the phone for ages

to Auntie Susan, but when Kitty came near she stopped speaking very quickly.

Then she took some time off work to go to the hospital, but when Kitty got worried and asked if she was ill, Mum laughed and said, 'No, I was just visiting somebody.' But Kitty just knew that wasn't true.

'Why do grown-ups think it's all right for THEM to tell little fibs?' she muttered, as Mum went out of the door.

Mum was a bit late picking Kitty up from school that night. She looked tired, and hardly spoke a word, all the way home. 'Are you all right, Mum?' Kitty asked.

'As well as can be expected,' said Mum, with a big sigh.

Then Dad came home from work with a big bunch of flowers for Mum. That was very strange because it wasn't her birthday, or Mothering Sunday, or their wedding anniversary.

'Dad's gone all sloppy,' whispered

Why me?

Daniel. 'It's *weird*!'

Then Mum burst into tears and flung her arms round Dad's neck.

'Mega-sloppy,' groaned Kitty. 'Something's wrong, I know it!'

She felt very worried indeed.

She beckoned Daniel to follow her out of the room, and when they were in the hall, she said, 'Well, Dan?'

'Well what?' he asked.

'Don't you think there's something funny going on?'

'Sort of,' said Dan.

'Well, will you come back in there with me and say we want to be told?'

'OK – safety in numbers!' grinned Dan.

The two children went back into the sitting room to find Mum and Dad sitting together on the sofa, holding hands.

'We want you to tell us . . .' Kitty began.

Kitty and friends

'We want to tell you both . . .' Mum began.

Then she stopped, looked at Dad – and started to giggle! It was so strange that Kitty began to feel rather cross. There's nothing worse than feeling left out of a secret.

'Well, go on!' she shouted.

'It's like this, love,' said Dad, 'Mum and me, we're . . . Well you aren't going to believe this, kids, but . . .'

'I'm expecting a baby,' said Mum, looking a bit shy.

Why me?

'Really?' said Daniel.

'WHAT?' shouted Kitty.

'Are you sure?' asked Dan.

'You *can't* be,' said Kitty.

'Well, I must say we were a bit surprised,' said Mum. 'I couldn't believe it at first, and I felt worried. But now I'm really happy.'

'We both are,' said Dad.

'Can I earn baby-sitting money?' asked Daniel.

'Not for a while. You have to be fourteen,' smiled Dad.

'Wow – it's really nice!' said Dan. 'I hope it's a boy – then I'll be able to play all the babyish games I used to like, but feel silly playing now. It'll be a good excuse!'

'Do you want us to have a girl, Kitty-Kat?' asked Dad.

'No,' was all Kitty said.

Then she rushed out of the room.

Upstairs in her bedroom Kitty sat for a

long time, just staring out of the window. When Mum called to say supper was ready, she went down slowly, and ate her meal in silence. Mum and Dad looked at each other and shrugged. Then there was a ring on the doorbell.

To Kitty's horror Auntie Susan, Uncle Joe and cousin Melissa stood on the step.

'We had to come round to say *congratulations*,' said Auntie Susan, 'now that you're sure. Ohhhh, it's *sooo* exciting.'

'I brought some bubbly,' winked Uncle Joe, holding up a wrapped bottle. There was a great noise of happiness, with everybody talking at once.

Kitty felt forgotten. But at least Melissa came over to her and said, 'So aren't you pleased you're going to have a little sister or brother?'

'Why me?' asked Kitty.

'I mean – it's for *them* to be pleased. It's *their* baby. What's it got to do with me?

Why me?

I mean – why should *I* care?' Kitty said, in a bored voice.

'I think that's mean,' said Melissa, tossing her curls, 'I love playing with my doll, and pretending she's a real baby."

'Yuk,' said Kitty.

'And with a real one, you'll be able to help dress it in pretty clothes, and change its little nappy,' squealed Melissa.

'Double yuk,' grunted Kitty.

'Kitty – I think you're being HORRID,' said Melissa, walking away.

Now the truth is, Kitty knew this was true. She hated feeling as she was feeling. When at last Auntie Susan and Uncle Joe took Melissa home, she didn't even go to the door to say goodbye. When she went upstairs to bed she knew Mum had a worried look on her face again.

Mum and Dad came up to say goodnight, but didn't come into Kitty's room – just stood at the door. Dad looked cross, Mum looked upset, but neither of them said anything. As they went away Kitty heard Dad whisper, 'She'll get used to the idea.'

I won't . . . I won't . . . Kitty thought.

Next day in school Kitty felt awful. She told Rosie and Anita her news, and wanted them to be on her side. But Rosie clapped her hands.

'Big families are great!' she said. 'I like babies!'

'Now you'll know what it's like to have little ones around the place,' smiled Anita.

'Oh thanks,' snorted Kitty.

Why me?

She tried to get some sympathy from William. After all, he was her very best friend in the whole world, she thought.

'Why me, Will?' she sighed.

'What do you mean?' asked William.

'I mean – why did this have to happen to ME? I like things as they are. I don't want a new baby, making a noise, mucking things up, taking Mr Tubs . . .'

'Why?' asked William.

'Well, would YOU like it? Why didn't it happen to you?'

''Cos it just didn't, that's all – but if it did, I'd be pleased,' said William. 'Honestly, Kit, I think you're being really silly!'

And with that he walked away.

That night Kitty walked home with William and his Mum, but didn't say a word to either of them. William's Mum didn't notice.

'Isn't it lovely news, about the new baby?' she said brightly. 'I went out today and bought your Mum a bright red baby suit – look!'

She pulled the little stretchy suit out of its bag and held it up for Kitty to see. But Kitty just nodded, and didn't even hold out her hand to touch it. Then William looked very cross indeed.

Once she was indoors, Kitty went straight upstairs, and when Mum popped her head around the door to ask if she would like a drink and a biscuit Kitty said NO – even though she was hungry and thirsty.

Mum came into her room and sat down on the bed. For a long time she didn't say anything; she just looked at Kitty with a sad little smile. It made Kitty feel small and bad inside. Then Mum said, 'Come on, pet, it's time we had one of our little talks.'

'What about?' said Kitty.

'You know!' smiled Mum. 'Ever since you heard about the baby you've been in a sulk.'

Why me?

'No, I haven't,' Kitty said.

Mum laughed. 'Oh, Kit-bag, do you think I'm blind? Don't spoil things, love – please. I feel so happy and so does Dad. Why can't you be happy with us?'

'Babies make a lot of noise at night . . . and . . . it might take my toys . . . and things like that,' mumbled Kitty, going very red.

'Oh, Kitty – this has nothing to do with the baby. It's got everything to do with YOU. What is it? Are you scared I won't have enough love to go round? That's it, isn't it?'

When Kitty heard her Mum say exactly what she had been thinking, but hadn't dared to admit – not even to herself – she burst into tears and rushed to sit on Mum's lap.

'There . . .' whispered Mum, stroking her shaggy head. 'You're still my baby, Kit – you know that? That won't stop, just because there'll be a new baby and you're getting to be a big girl. So there's no need to be jealous.'

'Promise?'

Mum laughed. 'This time I can make a real promise,' she said, 'as long as you make me a promise too.'

'What's that?' Kitty asked.

'Well, when the baby's born I want you to take on a very important job.'

'What's that?' asked Kitty, looking very pleased.

'I want you to teach it to talk,' said Mum.

'Why me?'

'Because,' said Mum, 'you're the very best at all the words every baby needs to know, as soon as possible. Do you know what they are?'

Why me?

Kitty grinned, jumped down and stood with her hands on her hips.

'Course I know,' she shouted with glee. 'There's . . . *I don't want to*! And *it's not fair*! And *but you promised*! And *I can't find it*! And . . .'

'Won't it be fun, Kitty?' smiled Mum.

'Yes – I can teach baby to be as naughty as I am,' Kitty laughed.

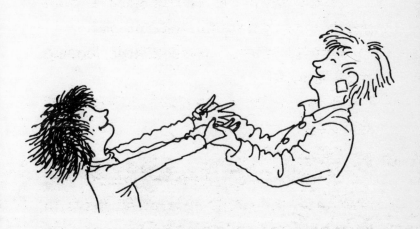